GAME ON, RYAN!

story by Ryan kaji

An imprint of Simon & Schuster Children's Publishing Division
New York London Toronto Sydney New Delhi
1230 Avenue of the Americas, New York, New York 10020
This Simon Spotlight edition December 2022

For more information about special discounts for bulk purchases, please contact Simon & Schuster Special Sales at 1-866-506-1949 or business@simonandschuster.com.
Manufactured in the United States of America 1122 LAK
2 4 6 8 10 9 7 5 3 1
ISBN 978-1-6659-2635-5

Hi, I'm Ryan! Today I'm going to play video games with Combo Panda. Alpha Lexa, Peck, and Gus the Gummy Gator are joining us too. What kind of games do you like to play?

We've all arrived at Combo Panda's house, but he's nowhere to be found. I wonder where he went?

Oh no, Combo's in trouble! He said he was at the end of the game, which means that we're going to have to beat the whole game to rescue him. Lucky for us, playing video games is exactly what we're here to do!

Everyone has brought their own lucky gaming controllers

Alpha Lexa has decorated her joysticks with heart-shaped stickers.

Peck's controller feels icy cold to the touch.

Gus has a controller with buttons that are squishy, like yummy gummies!

I'll borrow Combo's controller, which looks just like him.

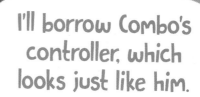

Turn to the back of the book to find your very own Red Titan controller! You'll use the controller throughout the story to help us beat the game.

The flower launched us high into the air, and now we're falling, falling, falling!

Can you turn your controller upside down so we can land on our feet?

Phew! We landed safely, but our characters are still feeling a little dizzy from the fall.

Turn the controller right side up again so they can regain their balance.

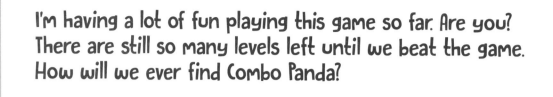

I'm having a lot of fun playing this game so far. Are you? There are still so many levels left until we beat the game. How will we ever find Combo Panda?

Maybe there's a shortcut!

Good thinking, Peck! Can you see any place that looks like a shortcut?

Once you find it, press the yellow button on your controller.

The tunnel led to a huge wall! How will we get past it?

Hmm, it looks like the wall is too high to jump over. What do we do now? We're stuck!

We did it! We broke through the wall and beat the game!
And look . . . there's Combo Panda, waiting for us at the finish line.

Hooray! Combo is safe and sound in the real world again.

Thanks for saving me! You have some real gaming skills!

ow that Combo's back, we can finally all ay together. But first I think it's time to ke a break and have a snack.

Yeah, all that waiting made me hungry! And after we take a break . . .

. . . we should play something that's not this game!

Thank you for helping me rescue Combo Panda from inside the game. Let's play together again soon!